Miss Beech unpacks some
books from a big box.
She stores the box in a corner.

"I will carry it out soon,"
she thinks.

The children all rush in and see the box.

Seth looks at the box.
"Hmmm," he thinks.
He sits in the box.

He pretends it is a red sports car.
"Vroom, vroom. I am the
winner!" shouts Seth.

Meg thinks the box is a boat. She ties her coat to a broom, for the sail.

The boat box sails in the wind.
Captain Meg stands at the helm.

The box sails into a storm.
It is tossed about.

"Help!" shouts Meg.
"The boat is sinking."

Meg hangs on to part of the boat. She sees some sand and swims to it.

Ben is a crab on the sand.
The box is his shell.
He peeps out from under it.

Next Anna gets
into
the
box.

She flies around and then loops
the loop. The children all clap.

Miss Beech looks at the box again.
"Perhaps I *shall* keep the box,"
she thinks.